For Kayla Rose. May you shine like a star.
x – J. W.

For my two grandads,
Grandad Fair and Grandad Smith
xx – B. M. S.

First U.S. edition 2019

Library of Congress Catalog Card Number pending
ISBN 978-1-5362-0265-6

18 19 20 21 22 23 WKT 10 9 8 7 6 5 4 3 2 1

Printed in Shenzhen, Guangdong, China

This book was typeset in Old Claude.
The illustrations were created in mixed media.

Nosy Crow an imprint of Candlewick Press
99 Dover Street, Somerville, Massachusetts 02144

www.nosycrow.com
www.candlewick.com

Stardust

Jeanne Willis

illustrated by Briony May Smith

nosy
crow

An imprint of Candlewick Press

When I was little,
I wanted to be a star.

My sister was a star. Everybody said so.
But nobody said it to me.

When Mom lost her wedding ring,
I looked for it everywhere, but my sister found it.
Mom said she was a star and so did Dad.

When Nana showed us how to knit, the scarf I made for Granddad was full of holes.

But the scarf my sister made for Nana wasn't.

"It's perfect. You little star!"
said Nana.

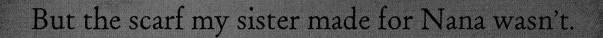

When we entered a costume competition,
Granddad said I looked amazing.
He said I might win. But . . .

I didn't.

My sister won.

Granddad dried
my eyes.

Later, Granddad found me gazing up at the sky.
There were thousands of stars. I made a wish.

I wished I was a star.

And Granddad said, "You are!"
Then he told me this story:
"Once upon a time,
there was . . .

NOTHING.

No sun. No moon. No world.

No trees. No creatures. Just darkness.

But then...

BANG!

Twinkle, twinkle.

The first star was born.

Then another

and another

and another

until ...

there were billions of stars, which

were brilliant and beautiful.

And there were planets, too.

With moons and mountains.

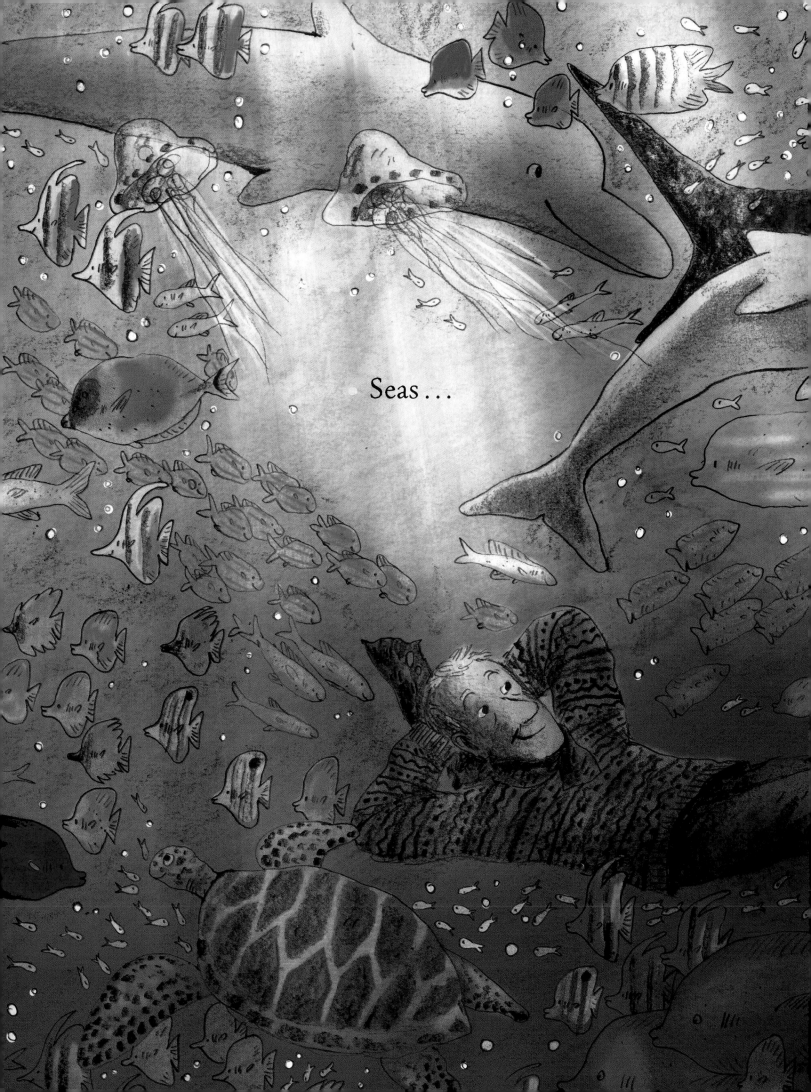

Seas...

and trees . . .

flowers and animals . . .

birds and butterflies . . .

BIG sisters and little sisters!"

"Everything and everyone is made of
stardust," said Granddad.
"But when will I sparkle?" I asked.
"When will I shine?"

"You already do!" Granddad replied.
"Remember that your sister isn't the only one
made of stardust. You just shine in different ways."

I did shine.

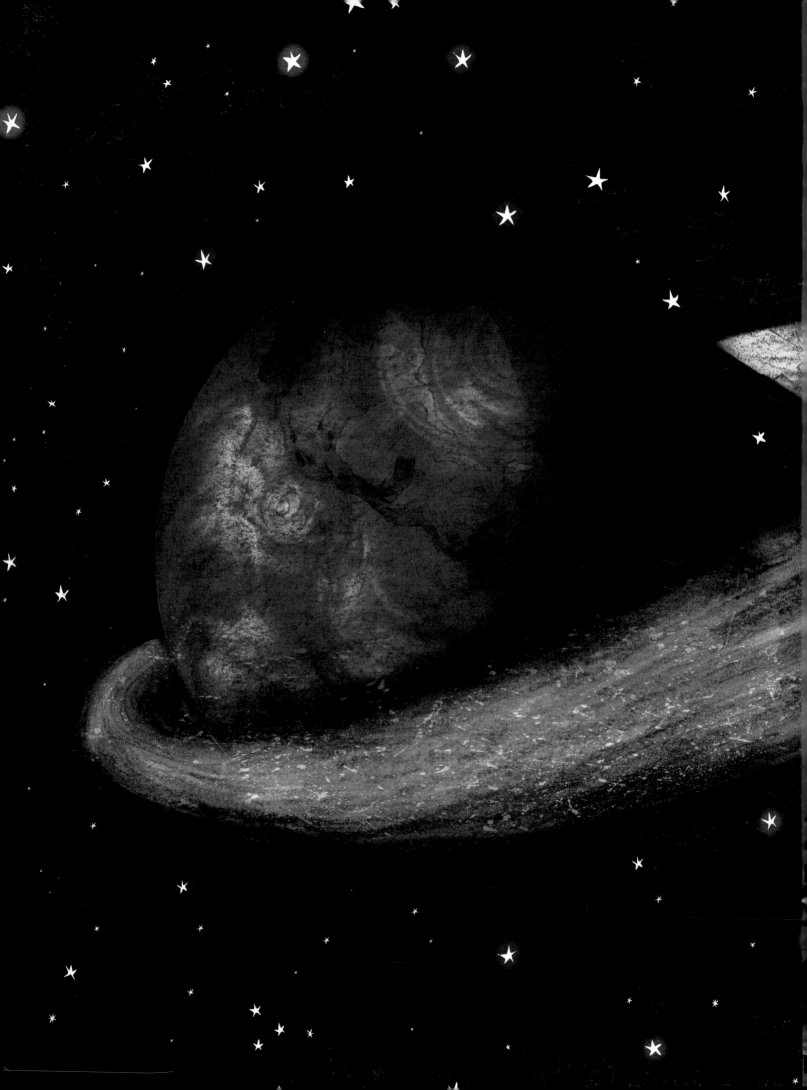

Shine in your own way.

Because, remember ...

you are made of stardust, too.